WINTER HARVEST

Jane Chelsea Aragon
Illustrated by Leslie Baker

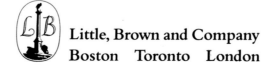
Little, Brown and Company
Boston   Toronto   London

This edition published in Great Britain in 1990 by
Little, Brown and Company (UK) Limited
Beacon House, 30 North End Road, London W14 0SH

ISBN 0-316-88843-5

A CIP catalogue record for this book is available from the
British Library

10 9 8 7 6 5 4 3 2 1

Printed in Belgium by Proost, Turnhout

For my parents
—*J.C.A.*

For Jon and Chris
—*L.B.*

On moonlit snow,
a deer waits for us.

Two fawns run to their mother.
In the pale light
a buck appears.

The wind blows.
It is cold under the stars.
The pond is frozen,
and the ground is hidden by snow.
My breath clouds the windowpane
as I look out.

Each winter evening,
when the deer cannot find anything to eat,
Papa and I bring them food.
After we have finished our supper
and we feel warm and full,
we are ready to go out into the cold night.

Papa and I fill the pail with grain and sweet corn,
which nourish the deer during the harsh winter.
Mama puts red apples into a basket
as my little brother looks on.

Papa takes his cap and coat from the rack,
and Mama helps me with mine.
The pail is too heavy for me to carry.
I carry the apples,
which taste of summer and early autumn.

I walk with Papa through falling snow
to the clearing beyond the trees.
Our boots sink into the snow
as we make our way to where the deer wait.
They remain still.
They know we will not harm them.

I help Papa scatter the grain and corn and apples
around the salt lick
that makes the deer thirsty for snow,
and helps them survive the long season.
We stand back and watch them.

When the fawns finish their supper,
they begin to play.
They leap into the air and kick up their heels.

They race around the slender grey trees.
They flip their white tails up.
They nip at one another affectionately.

Then they lie down to sleep under the pine tree
as snow falls silently around them.
Papa takes my hand and we walk back to our cottage,
to the warmth of our fire and our soft beds.

When I wake up early in the morning,
as the mist rises off the icy surface of the pond,
I can watch from my window
as the fawns and the doe follow the buck,
who listens for every sound.
They step lightly through the powdery snow.

The deer pause as they pass our cottage,
and the soft brown eyes of the fawns gaze at me.

They find shelter in the forest
and hide behind the trees.
They watch as Mama feeds the winter birds
and Papa shovels a path from our door.

As we go back inside
I turn to look at the deer,
but they have disappeared into
the woods until nightfall,
when they will return.